First Printing 1983

Heian International, Inc.
P.O. Box 2402
South San Francisco, CA 94080
U.S.A.

Originally published by Froebel-Kan Ltd., Tokyo
Translated by D.T. Ooka

ISBN: 0-89346-225-X

Printed in Japan

Little Bunny's Christmas Present

story by Setsuo Yazaki
illustrations by Ken Kuroi

Heian

Snow was falling, falling—soon it would be Christmas.

Little Bunny wrote a letter to Santa. "Please bring me a baby for Christmas," she wrote. "I want to be a big sister."

"Mail's here." called Mr. Rabbit Mailman as he delivered Bunny's letter to Santa Rabbit's house.

"Thank you, Mr. Mailman," said Santa Rabbit. He opened Bunny's letter and began to read.

"What's this, what's this? 'Please bring me a baby for Christmas.' Well now—isn't that cute! But what am I to do? I've never given a baby for Christmas! Oh dear…" worried Santa Rabbit as he stared at Bunny's letter.

Santa Rabbit decided to pay Santa Fox a visit to see if he could help.

"Bunny Rabbit says she wants a baby for Christmas," explained Santa Rabbit.

"That is a problem for you—babies are the one thing you can't give to anyone for a present," said Santa Fox.

"Actually, I had hoped that you would use your magical powers, Santa Fox, and turn a tree branch into a baby for me . . . but I guess you can't really do that, can you?"

"Of course not!" sputtered Santa Fox.

"Oh dear—what am I to do? Little Bunny seems to be waiting so eagerly for her Christmas present," fretted Santa Rabbit.

"Hmmm—maybe I'll visit Santa Mouse. He just might think of an answer for me." And so saying, Santa Rabbit set out for Santa Mouse's house.

"You say Bunny Rabbit wants a baby for Christmas? What a problem! Even though we mice have lots and lots of children, we can't very well give Bunny one of our babies," said Santa Mouse.

"That's true—oh, what am I to do? Little Bunny Rabbit is waiting so eagerly for her Christmas present!" moaned Santa Rabbit.

With Bunny's letter in hand, Santa Rabbit went to and fro, here and there. Finally, he came to Santa Goat's house.

"You say that Bunny Rabbit wants a baby for Christmas? What a problem—you could have given her anything else, but a baby...that's pretty impossible," mused Santa Goat.

"Oh, dear! What am I to do...I've got it! Santa Goat, won't you please eat this letter?" asked Santa Rabbit.

"Really, Santa Rabbit! That's no answer! Even if I eat Bunny's letter, that won't make her request go away!" scolded Santa Goat.

"That's true, Santa Goat. But what am I to do?"

"Hello..."

"Hello..."

"Hello..."

That evening Santa Rabbit was on the telephone
all night long. But he was not the only one.
Santa Fox, Santa Mouse, and Santa Goat were
all on the telephone, too. They called each of
their Santa friends to ask their advice about
Bunny Rabbit's letter.

The next day was Christmas Eve.

"Hello . . ."

"Hello . . ."

"Hello . . ."

"Hello . . ."

"Hello . . ."

The next day Bunny Rabbit danced about happily, shouting, "Merry Christmas, Merry Christmas! Will Santa Rabbit be here soon?"

Next to her bed that night, Bunny Rabbit hung a toy baby carriage instead of a stocking for Santa Rabbit to fill.

Soon she dropped off to sleep.

"Oh dear, oh dear...what shall I do? Bunny Rabbit will be so disappointed when she finds out she can't have a baby for Christmas..." Santa Rabbit was still in a quandary as he stood atop the Rabbit Family's roof.

"Santa Rabbit...!" A call came floating through the still night air.

"Oh! What are you all doing here?" asked Santa Rabbit.

"We were worried about you so we came to see if we could help," replied Santa Rabbit's friends.

"Thank you so much, everyone!"

Little Bunny Rabbit's eyes popped open. She'd been awakened by the Santas' voices.

"What can that be?" she wondered as she got out of bed, put on her slippers, and went over to the window.

When she pushed the curtain back and peeked out, she gasped, "Oh, my!"

"Oooh—how wonderful! Our yard is full of Santas!" cried Bunny as she threw open the window.

"We're so sorry, Little Bunny," apologized the Santas, all looking very sad. "We can't give you a baby for Christmas."

"But look! I can give you a baby doll!" said Santa Rabbit.

Santa Fox chimed in, "And I can give you doll clothes!"

"And here are some toys!"

"How about a picture book?"

All the other Santas joined in with their gifts. "It's just that no one can give you a baby—not even Santa!"

"No baby? But I thought Santa would give me anything I asked for!"

Little Bunny became sadder and sadder. "I want a baby! Boo hoo..." sobbed Bunny.

Hearing Bunny's cries, Mother Rabbit came to her bedroom. "What's going on, Bunny?" she asked, as she opened the door.

"Goodness gracious! Look at all those Santas!" gasped Mother Rabbit when she looked out the window.

"I can explain this..." said Santa Rabbit. He then told Mother Rabbit all about Bunny's letter.

"Is that what happened?! I am so sorry, Santas. It must have been a terrible problem for all of you," said Mother Rabbit.

"Now look here, Bunny. A baby is the one thing that Santa cannot give you for Christmas," said Mother Rabbit.

"Why not?" asked Bunny.

"That's because a baby is the most precious treasure that anyone can have."

"Then who gives babies?"

"Babies are given by M-O-T-H-E-R. Bunny, do you really want a baby?" asked Mother Rabbit.

"Yes, Mommy. I want to be a big sister!" replied Bunny.

"That's wonderful! Bunny—soon we're going to have a baby rabbit!" said Mother Rabbit.

"Honest?"

"Yes. Will you take good care of the baby?" asked Mother Rabbit.

"Oh yes, yes, Mommy! I'll take very good care of the baby!" said Bunny.

"Now, Bunny, put your ear next to Mommy's stomach. Can you hear the baby rabbit?"

"Oh, yes! I can really hear a baby rabbit moving around, Mommy! I'm so happy!" cried Bunny.

"Hooray! Isn't that wonderful, Bunny? Your mommy is the best Santa in the world!" cheered all the Santas. "She can give you the one present that none of us can give you!"

"Well, now—it's time for us to be heading home," said one of the Santas.

Santa Rabbit said, "Goodbye, Bunny. I'll be back again next year!"

"Thank you, Santa. Next year I'll have become a good big sister to baby rabbit!" cried Bunny.

"Goodbye, Bunny!"

"Goodbye, Santa!"